THE
STONE LION

<small>WRITTEN AND ILLUSTRATED BY</small>

Bill Slavin

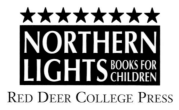

NORTHERN
LIGHTS BOOKS FOR CHILDREN

<small>RED DEER COLLEGE PRESS</small>

NORTHERN LIGHTS BOOKS FOR CHILDREN ARE PUBLISHED BY
Red Deer College Press
56 Avenue & 32 Street Box 5005
Red Deer Alberta Canada T4N 5H5

ACKNOWLEDGEMENTS
Edited for the Press by Tim Wynne-Jones.
Design by Esperança Melo.
Printed and bound in Canada by Quality Color Press for Red Deer
College Press.
Financial support provided by the Alberta Foundation for the Arts,
a beneficiary of the Lottery Fund of the Government of Alberta,
and by the Canada Council, the Department of Communications
and Red Deer College.

COMMITTED TO THE DEVELOPMENT OF CULTURE AND THE ARTS

CANADIAN CATALOGUING IN PUBLICATION DATA
Slavin, Bill
The stone lion
(Northern lights books for children)
ISBN 0-88995-154-3
I. Title.   II. Series.
PS8587.L43S76 1996 jC813'.54 C95-911052-6
PZ7.S53St 1996

*To Esperança
who gives me wings*

THE STONE LION
sat perched in its
aerie far above the city.
High on top of the
cathedral's bell tower it
crouched, great stone
wings folded along its
sides, gray eyes staring
out over the land.

Far below and across the square from the cathedral stood a silversmith's shop. In the shop worked a boy. The cathedral was the first thing the boy saw every morning as he rose at dawn to fold open the shop's shutters and stoke the fire in the forge. And it was the last thing he saw at night when, weary from the long day, he would close the window of the attic room against the coolness of the night and go to his bed.

All day the boy worked with pride at his bench, hammering out small silver ornaments that would be bought by pilgrims when they visited the cathedral. He would often look up from his work to the tower and the great stone lion high above. The boy knew that from where the lion perched one could see the distant village where his family lived.

Six months ago the boy had left his village to come to the city, apprenticed to his uncle to learn the silversmith's trade. The evening before he was to depart he had gone to his grandmother's bed to say good-bye. The boy was very close to his grandmother— she had looked after him since he was a baby while his mother and father worked in the fields. He loved to sit by the fire in the kitchen as she prepared the evening meal, and listen to her tell mysterious tales of the wood sprites and fairies that lived in the forest. But that was before his grandmother had become very ill. When he entered her room to say good-bye on the eve of his departure, the boy was worried he would not see her again.

His grandmother could see the worry on his face. "Look out the window," she said. "What do you see?"

"I see the village and the river," said the boy.

"And beyond?" asked the grandmother. "What is it that you see beyond?"

The boy lifted his eyes past the hills to a great spire in the far-off distance. "The tower of the cathedral," said the boy.

"When I was a girl," said the grandmother, "I lived in the city. I was apprenticed to a dressmaker, a hard, unhappy woman with a heavy pair of cloth shears which she would strike me with when I fumbled a stitch. I was very sad in the city until I discovered the stone lion. From his back you can see over the entire countryside. I would climb to the top of the tower and lie there for hours, imagining what it would be like to live out there in those green fields. And sometimes I would doze off and dream of a field by a stream, dream I was lying in the cool, green grass with the sun filtering down upon me through the leaves of an old oak that grew in the field. And the dream was so real that when I awoke I would wonder where I had been, to which of those far-off green fields I had traveled."

The boy smiled at the old woman's fanciful ideas. "The place couldn't have been real if you only dreamed it," he said.

"Oh, but I know it was real," replied his grandmother. "And in the dream I would sometimes hear a voice. 'I know this place, too,' the voice would say. 'Someday, when time and the moon are full we will travel there together.'"

But the boy only half-listened to his grandmother's tale. A thought had occurred to him. "Could you see our village from the spire?" he asked.

"Oh, yes," smiled his grandmother, "as clearly as I can see the spire from this bed. So you see, we won't be so far apart." And with that she hugged him and gave him a kiss good-bye.

The boy's sleep was troubled that night. He awoke before dawn to the light of a single candle and his father's hand on his shoulder, raising him for the long day's journey to the city.

That was six months ago. Winter had come and gone. A friend of his father's who had traveled the long distance to the city market had told his uncle that the boy's grandmother's health had worsened. The boy worried for her and had asked his uncle if he could travel to see her.

"It is a full day's journey and the same to come back," his uncle had said. "I am too busy to take the time to accompany you, and you are too young to make the trip by yourself. I am sorry, but we will have to wait until business is slower."

So whenever the boy had a moment, during the noon hours when the shop was closed or late in the evenings after the last of the pilgrims had wandered from the square, he would climb the three hundred and sixty-five steps to the top of the bell tower, scramble onto the back of the stone lion and look into the distance. His eye would travel the familiar route along the river, which winked in the sun as it wound between the rounded green hills to his village, so small and far away. There in the village, the boy knew, would be his grandmother looking out to the cathedral's tower.

One night, soon after his father's friend had brought word of
his grandmother, the boy had a dream. In the dream he saw
his grandmother, white hair unbound and billowing in the wind.
The stars were rushing by, and there was a great whooshing of air,
like the sound of the bellows in the blacksmith's shop. Then his
grandmother called his name, and he woke to the sound of her
voice. He lay awake in bed, unable to get back to sleep. He thought
of his grandmother and how badly he wished he could go home.
Finally, he got up from his bed and quietly left his uncle's house.
He ran across the square to the cathedral, dark and shadowy
against the moon, and entered the door at the base of the tower.

In the darkness he climbed the three hundred and sixty-five steps to the roof. He scrambled onto the back of the stone lion and looked out to the distant hills where his village slept in the shadows.

"Oh, lion," he said, his fingers curling into the stone mane, "I wish I could get home!"

And then, beneath his chest, he felt the stone heave. "I miss my home, too," the boy heard a low voice say. "I miss the cool grass on my flanks and the warm earth against my belly. I miss the rustle of leaves over my head."

The boy was amazed. "You were a real lion?" he asked.

"No," replied the lion. "I was a stone in a farmer's field. A beautiful stone, a stone fit for the sculptor's chisel."

"And now we are both trapped here in this city," said the boy. "And I suppose I have about as much chance to go home as you do."

"I have traveled far in my lifetime, long before I made this most recent journey down the river to this city to be shaped to the form you see me in now," said the stone lion. "In the passing of the ages I have sat perched on the tops of mountains and have tumbled down into plains. I have been carried by ice to the bottoms of oceans and then thrust back onto land. So I know it is true that nothing is forever and all things are possible under the moon. But it was human hands that dragged me from the earth, gave me this new form, and perched me one step from heaven. And it will be a human who will take me home."

"But how?" asked the boy.

"There are many paths home. The man who mixed the mortar that binds me to this tower was, like most humans, in a hurry. The mortar is weak and crumbling, and paves the short way home. Someday, when time and the moon are full, it will break. . . ."

The words triggered a memory of the story his grandmother had told him the day he had left for the city. The lion had just spoken exactly the same words as the voice she had heard in her dreams. "It was you who spoke to my grandmother!" he cried.

"Ah, so the little girl is your grandmother," the stone lion sighed. "How quickly people grow old. . . ."

"You promised to take her to your home."

"Did I, now?"

"She needs you."

"But the mortar still holds me here," said the lion.

"What if I climbed onto the back of your head?" asked the boy. "Would my weight be enough to dislodge you?"

"You would fall to your death," said the lion.

The boy peered down, down to the cathedral square, and for a moment he wavered. Then suddenly he remembered his own dream and the great whooshing of air, which sounded like bellows.

"But the sculptor gave you wings!" cried the boy. "You can fly! I know you can. You carried her in my dream!"

"Do you believe this dream was true?" asked the stone lion. "Do you trust it enough to help me escape this tower?"

"If it will take me to my grandmother," said the boy. And so the boy inched his way out onto the head of the lion. The stone creaked and groaned, and little bits of mortar broke from the tower and tumbled down into the darkness below. The boy tightened his grip on the lion's mane and shifted his weight forward. Suddenly, there was a great crack, and the lion lurched, breaking loose and plunging boy and lion down end over end toward the cathedral square. The ground came rushing toward them, and the boy squeezed his eyes shut against what seemed to be certain death.

"Spread your wings!" the boy shouted, and he felt the powerful wings of the lion surge beneath him. A moment later he glanced down to see the roofs of the houses spiral away as they climbed up, up into the starry night.

"We did it!" shouted the boy as the cool night wind whistled through his hair.

"We're free!" roared the lion, so loud that people in the city rose from their beds and closed their shutters against the coming storm. "Where shall we fly?" asked the lion to the boy. "To the pyramids of Tikal or the domed towers of Babylon? Tonight, all things are possible!"

"Take me home!" shouted the boy, and with a thrust of the stone lion's massive wings they turned to the east and toward the boy's village.

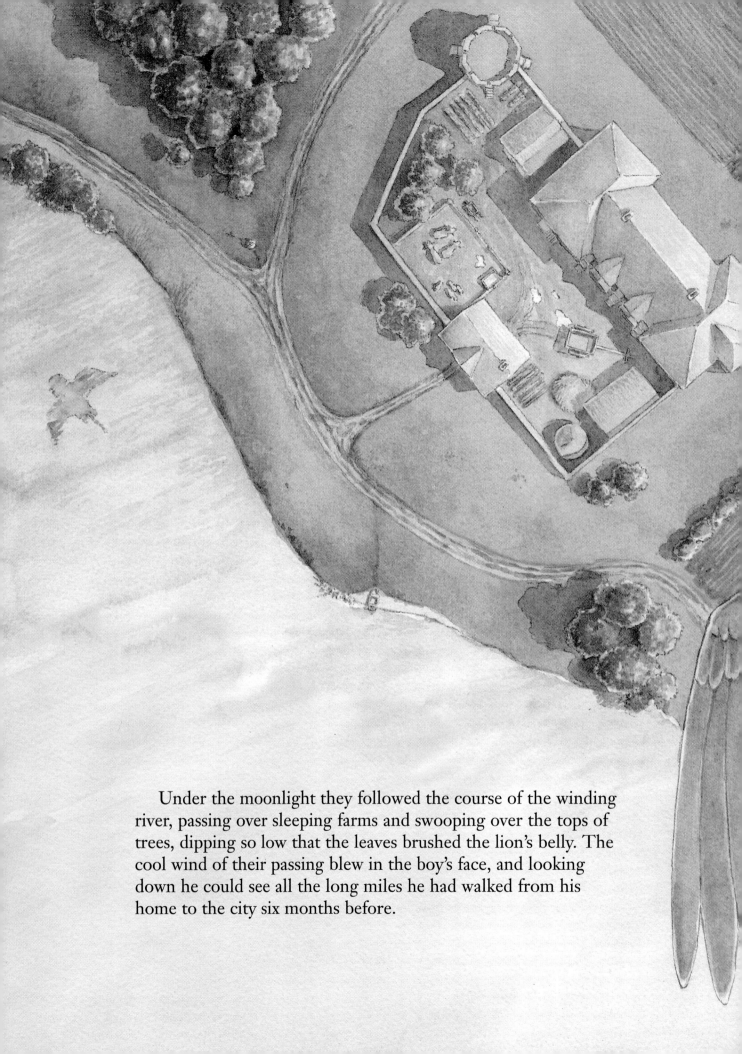

Under the moonlight they followed the course of the winding river, passing over sleeping farms and swooping over the tops of trees, dipping so low that the leaves brushed the lion's belly. The cool wind of their passing blew in the boy's face, and looking down he could see all the long miles he had walked from his home to the city six months before.

The boy's village appeared as they soared over the last hill of their journey, and the lion flew down and landed by the well in the middle of the village. He folded his wings as the boy slid off his back and down to the ground.

"I have to go to my grandmother," the boy said.

"I will wait for you here," called the lion softly, standing as still and silent as a statue again.

The house was in darkness, but the door leading to the garden was always left open. The dog, asleep in the backyard, opened one eye and started to growl as the boy climbed over the fence, but then recognizing his smell, the dog went back to his own dreams. The boy quietly lifted the latch of the back door and let himself in. He tiptoed through the sleeping house, past the embers glowing in the fireplace and up the stairs to the loft. By the light of the moon he could see his parents and sister in the big bed as he made his way to the far end of the loft where his grandparents slept. A candle was burning behind the curtain, and when the boy pulled it aside he could see his grandfather, face lined with concern and exhaustion, asleep in a chair by his grandmother's bed. His grandmother's eyes were closed, but then she stirred, and she saw the boy standing there.

"I had a dream you would come," she said.

"I had a dream you called me," said the boy. "I flew here on a stone lion."

"Ah," said his grandmother. "You came for me."

The boy helped his grandmother from the bed. She turned toward the boy's grandfather, still sleeping in the chair, and lay her hand gently on his forehead. The brow smoothed, and the lines around his eyes softened.

"Should we wake him?" asked the boy.

"No, let him sleep," said his grandmother. "He and I have already said our good-byes." They descended the steps from the loft. As they left the house and walked toward the waiting lion, the grayness left his grandmother's face, and it shone with the cool, blue light of the moon.

The stone lion smiled as the grandmother approached. "I remember a time not so long ago when a young girl used to climb onto my back at the top of the cathedral tower and dream of the countryside."

"And I remember, in my dreams, that a voice promised to take me to that place by a stream. A place I had never been but had known all my life," replied the grandmother.

The boy lifted his grandmother, frail and light as a bird, onto the back of the lion and then climbed on behind.

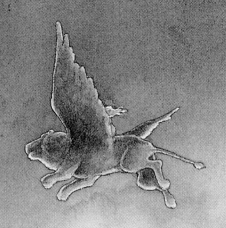

The lion once more spread his wings and sprang into the sky. Time and the stars spun by in the rushing wind of their flight as they returned the way they had come.

The first pale light of dawn was just appearing behind the cathedral when the lion touched down softly in the square. As the boy kissed his grandmother good-bye for the last time, she slipped a locket from around her neck and handed it to him.

"Thank-you for coming," she said, smiling. "I have a long journey ahead of me, and I was glad for your company for the first part of the way."

The boy turned and hugged the lion good-bye as well, and then stood watching as they soared up above the tower of the cathedral and winged away into the sky, toward the distant hills. The boy remained there for a long time, watching, and then turned and entered his uncle's home. He closed the windows of his attic room against the chill breeze that came at dawn and went to sleep.

❦❦❦

The boy straightened the tools on his workbench and damped down the fire in the forge. It had been a busy day in the cathedral square. There was still much talk about the stone lion's mysterious disappearance from the top of the bell tower. The people whispered that the bishop had it removed in the dead of night to make room for a statue of himself. It was rumored that the stone carver had already received a commission for such a statue.

Earlier that afternoon a tinker had arrived in the city with news from the boy's village that his grandmother had died peacefully three nights ago in her sleep. His uncle had offered to close the shop and travel with the boy to his village the next day, but the boy told him it was not necessary.

Winter would arrive in a few more months, and then there would be time to visit his family. And thinking this, his hand rose to his grandmother's locket hanging beneath his tunic. He glanced at the cathedral once more before lowering and fastening the shutters at the front of the shop.